Oliver Finds His Way

For Amelia — P. R.

For my brother, Rob — C. D.

ISBN 0-439-58910-X

Text copyright © 2002 by Phyllis Root.
Illustrations copyright © 2002 by Christopher Denise. All rights reserved.
Published by Scholastic Inc., 557 Broadway, New York, NY 10012,
by arrangement with Candlewick Press. SCHOLASTIC and associated
logos are trademarks and/or registered trademarks of Scholastic Inc.

12 11 10 9 8 7 6 5 4 3 2 1   3 4 5 6 7 8/0

Printed in the U.S.A.   40

First Scholastic printing, October 2003

This book was typeset in Kennerley.

The illustrations were done in pastels and charcoal on paper.

Oliver Finds His Way

Phyllis Root

illustrated by
Christopher Denise

SCHOLASTIC INC.
New York Toronto London Auckland Sydney
Mexico City New Delhi Hong Kong Buenos Aires

While Mama hangs the wash out
and Papa rakes the leaves,
Oliver chases a big yellow leaf…

down the hill,

around a clumpy bush,

under a twisty tree,

and all the way

to the edge of the woods.

Oliver looks for the leaf.

No leaf.

Oliver looks for his house.

No house.

"Mama? Papa?" Oliver calls,
and he begins to run.

He runs to a tree.

That's not the twisty tree!

He runs to a bush.

That's not the clumpy bush!

All alone at the
edge of the woods,
Oliver starts to cry.
Oliver is lost.

Oliver cries
and cries
and cries.

But he is still lost.

Oliver rubs his nose
and tries to think.

He thinks
and thinks
and thinks.

All alone at the
edge of the woods,
Oliver has an idea.

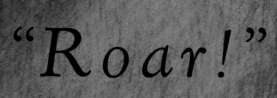

"*Roar!*"

"*Roar!*"

"Roar!"

From far away,
under a tree,
around a bush,
and up a hill,
Oliver hears Mama
roaring back.
Oliver hears Papa
roaring back.

Oliver runs and runs . . .
under the twisty tree,

around the clumpy bush,

up the hill,
all the way
to his very own house
with a pile of leaves
and wash on the line.

All the way
to Mama and Papa
with tumble-down hugs...

and a big yellow leaf
just for Oliver.